GRIND

JAMES JOSIAH

Copyright © 2020 James Josiah

Cover art by Lucy Onions

ISBN: 978-1-9163441-4-3

For Beryl

*Who gave me a home when I didn't think I
deserved one.*

*"Wisdom comes alone through
suffering"*

\- Aeschylus

ONE

"You know Jackie? Jackie? Jackie from accounts Jackie? Yeah you do, you know Jackie. Jackie, Jackie. Barbara's sister? Barb. Big Barb. Big Barb who works in the canteen? She was knocking off Gary from the warehouse behind her husband's back? I'm sure her bloke is called Colin or Clive or Carl or Craig or Greg, something starting with C anyway. Their dad, Trevor, Trev, Big Trev, Big Trev the trucker, the one who used to work in transport before he had the accident and then retired early when he got that big compo payout. Val reckons he got a hundred and twenty five grand. All that money and they still live up on The Barons? Says it all if you ask me. No class. Anyway I heard Jackie saying to Sarah that she had told Paul, you know Paul? Started as a picker before he got the stores team leader job, which everyone knows he only got

because he was screwing Janet. Anyway Jackie was telling Sarah that she had told Paul to stay away from Claire so really he only has himself to blame if you ask me."

No one asked her. No one would ever ask her. Her opinion, on anything you could ever think of, means nothing to anyone. Not that she doesn't let that stop her forming one and then informing everyone within earshot as to what it is. As far as I can tell, she knows (or at least thinks she knows) everyone that works at Finnister's. And everyone knows, or at least has heard of, her. Every place has a rumour mill but there has never been one run so efficiently and so utterly ruthlessly by one single person. It's not even like she has a position of power. No one works for her. She has no influence on anything, at all. Anywhere. She is just a packer. Just another body at the end of the conveyor. Just another nobody. Just like you. Just like me.

I think abcut shooting her in the back of the head. Just walking up behind her and ending her pathetic existence. Point blank. No messing about. No doubts, worries or risks of her surviving. Putting her out of her, mine, and hopefully other people's misery once and for all. After all I can't be the only person whose life would be better without her in it. It would be easy. It would be so, so easy. I could do it in a heartbeat and genuinely feel no remorse.

I'd honestly be doing the world a favour. The only problem is if anything it would be too easy. Too quick. Too clean. At the very least she deserves to be able to form an opinion on what is happening to her and why it is. She has earnt that if nothing else.

She hasn't even noticed that I haven't acknowledged her, or her rambling, let alone even tried to get a word in edgeways before one of the nurses comes in and thankfully interrupts her. It's Lena, the Polish one with the Temazepam glazed gaze. She always smells of cheap perfume and minty fresh chewing gum, but neither ever mask the smell of stale smoke that clings to her hair. You'd think a nurse would know better than to smoke, wouldn't you? I bet she has the nerve to tell her patients that they shouldn't. Still, we all have our vices, don't we?

Lena asks Mother how I'm doing today. Mother reluctantly stops talking at me and says that Lena should surely be telling her how I am. After all that is meant to be her job isn't it? Lena gives Mother what I imagine to be a well-practiced, curt smile that has "Fuck you" beautifully stamped all over it, if you know where to look. And I do know where to look. I have the exact same smile myself.

Lena asks me how much pain I'm in, on a scale of one to ten. Ten being the worst pain I can possibly imagine. I consider trying to tell her about the headache that feels like it's tearing my soul in two. I glance down and try not to think about my splintered ribs and how every breath sets my lungs on fire. Instead I imagine dunking my face into a deep fat fryer and cooking my brain. I think about pushing my hands into a meat grinder, gouging my eyes out with a teaspoon, driving rusty nails through my feet, putting cigarettes out on my nipples, injecting diesel into my veins. I think about all of those things instead of telling the truth, because the truth never sets us free. The truth will trap you. The truth will bog you down, suck you dry and kill you. So, I lie. I always lie. Lying is what I do best. I give her my best smile, showing her the few teeth I have left in my shattered skull. I flash her my bloodshot baby blue black eyes and shakily, hold up two fingers.

She smiles back, kindly masking her disgust at the state of me, and tells me I don't have to be brave. She says that she'll pop down in a bit with a few painkillers and scribbles something in my notes. All I can think is how she won't be coming back with the pills I don't want or even really need. I mean it's only a little bit of excruciating pain isn't it? When did that ever hurt anyone? She'll pocket them and glide through the rest of her shift in a blissfully numb daze. Well you knock yourself out, doll. I need to be bright eyed and bushy tailed and it seems like nothing quite focuses the mind like a ridiculous amount of pain. As soon as Lena is gone Mother starts again.

"Bloody typical, can barely speak a word of bloody English, stinking of fags and God knows what else. She's probably drunk, you know how they like a drink. Three days you've been in here and I've still yet to see a white face let alone meet anyone with a name that doesn't sound like they are clearing their throat. It's no wonder this country is in the state it is when we're letting creatures like that in just because they say they are qualified. And to what standard are they even qualified to? I remember when the NHS was the pride of the country and the envy of the world. Look at it now, it's bloody disgraceful. Still, that's what you get for ever letting the lefties into power. I told everyone they would be pissing all the money up the wall and opening the doors for all to come in but did they listen? Did they hell as like. All they ever think about is themselves. No sense of community anywhere anymore. Everyone wants a hand out these days. No one wants to work for anything, not like you had to in my day. Me and your father, God rest his soul, bought our first house when we were twenty three. Well he was twenty seven but can you imagine a twenty year old having the gumption to pull their finger out of their arse to get themselves on the property ladder

these days? Bone idle the lot of them. I'll tell you something, you should count yourself lucky we raised you the way we did. Taught you right from wrong, the value of money and the importance of an honest, hard day's work."

She barely pauses for breath. It's just an unrelenting constant stream of ill thought out nonsense. Every word out of her mouth is somehow worse than the one before it. All I want is for her to shut the fuck up and fuck the fuck off out of my life. Forever. All I want is to be left alone with my pain. After all, what's the point of all this suffering if I can't revel in it?

"Anyway like I was saying Jackie, Jackie from accounts Jackie, you know Jackie. Jackie was telling Sarah how she had told Paul to stay away from Claire. She's no good that girl, rotten to the core, just like her mother. The entire family are nothing but scum and have been for as long as anyone can remember. I don't even understand how her mum had all of those kids given the time Eric spent locked up. Well the rumours always were she was on the game and no one knows who their real dads are, not even her. She always looked the type if you ask me. Still does to this day as well, skirt up round her arse, showing off her varicose veins. Flaunting it down The Coach and Horses. Absolutely no shame at all, that one. She's a brazen hussy.

Mutton dressed as lamb is putting it politely if you ask me, the dirty fucking slut."

I close my eyes and try to retreat into myself. Find nirvana and float away. Just phase her out. Maybe I should have had those pills after all, they would surely help. I would try to grit my teeth, but there aren't many left and my jaw still feels like it's going to fall off any time it moves or even if I just think about it for too long. I lick my lips and taste blood. Somehow, she is still talking and still hasn't actually reached any sort of point. It's too much. I can't take it anymore. I admit defeat and finally let out the words that have been burning the back of my throat since Dad left us all those years ago.

"Mother, please, for the love of God and all that is holy, shut the fuck up, for once in your cunt life."

She stops. She actually stops talking for once in her fucking life. There is this glorious moment of pure, unadulterated silence and for a second, I worry that I may have actually gone deaf. I can't believe that I've done it and that it worked. Euphoria washes over me. I have never been so happy. She looks at me, I can see the fear in her eyes, and it is frankly exquisite. Mother stands up and it looks like she is going to leave. Just walk out of the door and never come back. I have dreamed about this moment for all of my life so I try to sit up so I can really savour the moment as it's something I want to remember until my dying day. She walks to the door, leans against the frame. Takes a deep breath and screams down the ward for someone to come quickly as I'm distressed.

There is a flurry of activity, I'm poked and prodded from all angles. Lights are flashed into my eyes. They are all calling my name and asking if I can hear them. And I can, but in their blind panic, they don't seem to be hearing me. Lena floats into the fray and drawls that she was just on her way to administer some pain relief. Anna, the head honcho, says I clearly need something a little stronger. There is a sharp sting. A quick prick. Ice runs through my veins and everything melts away into glorious, delicious, blackness.

Every city and every town has an area like it. Even the village my grandparents live in has a street you wouldn't want to find yourself down alone in the middle of the night. So why was I there? I wasn't looking for trouble, I never go looking for trouble. I've never been in trouble my whole life. I was trying to help. No matter what anyone tells you or how bad it looks and sounds, I just wanted to help.

I had nothing but good intentions. I want you to remember that. I need you to remember that.

Ok so I was looking for her. I'll admit to that. It's not a crime. I'm not a stalker. No laws were being broken. Or not by me anyway. I just wanted to see if she was around and who knows I may have even plucked up the courage to actually speak to her. Her profile says her name is Darcy but her real name is either Tessa or Dawn or Donna or Mandy. At least that's what she's called in some of the clips I have found of her in action. A lot of them don't even give her a name. They just label her, as if she is nothing more than an object of desire. Chubby milf, fat slag, dirty old bitch with massive tits, busty mature whore, cock hungry cunt. Of course, I've watched them all. Some more than once. Each time she looks into the camera you can see the panic in her eyes. The desperation. The almost frantic, desperate and urgent need to please whoever it is that films her. The one that makes her do the things she does. She's got these beautiful blue grey eyes and it feels like you could lose your soul if you stared into them for too long. So, I was looking for her, I'll admit to that much. But I wasn't a punter. I wasn't some sad sack looking to get their end away. I just wanted to help. I just wanted to help her. You can't tell me that makes me a bad person. If anything, I'm the real victim.

TWO

"What you have to remember, doctor, is that they have always been like this. Had the chickenpox as a child and just lay there not even trying to get better. Just wallowing in their own misery as if that has ever helped anyone. Never known what's for the best in the long run so you push on with whatever you think is best and I'll make sure all the paperwork gets signed properly and we can all start getting on with our lives again."

We're seeing Jenny, the consultant, and I know I'm meant to be paying attention. I know this is important. I know this is all very, very important and that I really should be listening to her, but what's the point? They asked if I wanted Mother here with me for this and I tried to say no. I really did. Admittedly it was more to try and spite her than as a display of me being anything like a functioning adult. I'm not saying I need her here. I can think of nothing worse than having to rely on her ever again. But at the very least, if she takes charge I can try and hide from the grim reality ahead of me. Jenny keeps saying words like "*reconstructive surgery, skin grafts, bone grafts, implants, bridges, breaking and resetting. Pain management, prolonged recovery times but fairly minimal risks.*"

Eventually it all just becomes white noise and I think about how we shouldn't really be on first name terms. How wholly unprofessional it all is. I know she is trying to put me at ease with her well-practiced soothing, caring, voice and touchy-feely over familiarity but she just comes across like one of those cool, young, trendy, fresh out of uni teachers who tell the kids to call them Dave, or Tristan, or Kylie. The type of teacher who never earns the respect of their students. The type of teacher you see in the papers after they are caught in the stationary cupboard with a sixth former. The type of person who sets out wanting to change the world and ends up ruining everything they touch. I wonder if it is too late for me to retrain?

Somehow, they are still talking and all I can think about is setting Jenny on fire. I think about the warm *whoomph* as the flames catch. I think about toasting marshmallows over her smoldering corpse. I think about cutting slices of flesh from her thighs and frying them off in salted butter and freshly foraged wild garlic. I think about the spit and crackle in the pan as her fat starts to crisp up.

She bursts my bubble by asking if I understand. If I need some time to let it all sink in. She says she knows it must be daunting. She has a kind smile and the warmth in her voice tells you she might actually mean what she says. But she doesn't know anything. Not really. She might be highly educated. She might have performed these procedures dozens of times before. But she doesn't know anything about me. About life. About Suffering. About pain. Not really. Not yet anyway.

I sign all of her consent forms without really reading them, because what other options do I have? It's not like they are doing any of this for fun now are they? There is a degree of cosmetic to the procedures but it's mainly all functional. There is a lot of talk about me being able to lead a normal life again. As if normal is anything to strive towards. As if I was ever normal to start with. I'll never be pretty. You'll always be able to see that something went very wrong in my life at some point. As far as I can tell, the scarring should be to the degree that it'll intrigue, and then hopefully upset small children. Strangers will stare but never dare to ask what happened to me. People will go home and tell their partners about the freak in the supermarket. I agree to allow the harvesting of my organs should the worst happen, secretly hoping that it does, and that any healthy and undamaged organs they manage to find overpower their host body and my spirit or soul or whatever is left after we die, lives on to fight another day.

There is part of me, buried deep down inside, that likes the idea of taking over someone's life. Completely and utterly dominating them, making every little decision for them. What and when and even if they eat or drink. Deciding if they can go to the toilet depending on how desperately they beg. Telling them what to wear, where to go and when to be there. Have them ask my permission for every little mundane task. It's not a sexual thing. Not in the slightest. I'm not a deviant. I just want someone to want me. I want someone to need me. I just want to ruin someone. I want to take something fresh and new, something full of promise and hope and then I want to break it beyond all recognition. It's not too much to ask for is it?

Jenny can sense she is losing me. She smiles her beautiful smile and I drink in her hope. I let her warmth and kindness nourish me and for a minute, even I believe that everything is going to work out fine. As if anyone in this life gets or deserves a happy ending. She says that I need some rest as if I have done anything other than lie around in bed for a fortnight. She says that I have a big day in the morning. She says that tomorrow is the first day of the rest of my life as if that isn't true for everybody. She says all of this and all I can think about is how she tastes. She asks if I have any questions and I just shrug my shoulders.

As she leaves, she shakes my hand and says that she'll see me on the other side. I grip tightly and hold her for a second or two too long, enjoying her touch and her politely stifled discomfort. She's not wearing a wedding ring but that doesn't mean anything anymore, does it? I lick my lips and taste blood.

After she and Mother leave the police come to see me. Again. The same two officers pop by every few days to see me. To see how I'm doing and if I can remember anything about the attack yet. I can remember every blow. Every screamed threat. Every warning. I can still feel that first delicious punch and then every kick that followed it. I can still hear the sound of my skull splitting as I hit the ground. I can still taste the damp grass of the verge they left me on. I can still smell the mud. But I've not said anything of any worth to them and I don't think I ever will. Because what's the point? They seem happy enough with my supposed memory loss. It doesn't seem to be hindering them in any way shape or form. If anything, it appears to be giving them some drive. A sense of purpose. I like that. I like that they need me to be helpless. Beyond hope. I wonder how much harder they would be working if I had had the decency to die? They keep showing me pictures of potential suspects and asking if I recognise any of them. I don't but I'd like to.

This gallery of rogues and miscreants keep me awake at night, in a good way, I mean. I want to find these men that the police think have the potential to have hurt men. These men that the police know could have hurt me. I want to find them, and I want them to use me. I want them to fulfil their darkest desires. I want to be their canvas, their muse, their blank slate. I want to sate their thirst and hunger. I want my utter destruction to be their redemption. I want to be a victim. I need to be a victim.

The officers always apologise, and I like that. They are always very, very, polite. Very professional. They are very earnest and very reassuring when they say that they are doing everything they can. They promise me that they will catch whoever did this to me and punish them to the full extent of the law. All I want to tell them is that I want to find them myself and shake them by the hands. Because as close as they came to killing me, I've never felt so alive and I want them to finish the job. I need them to and I want her to be there when it happens.

Her profile lists her email address and tells you the hours she works. It tells you where you can find her on the street if she hasn't already got a booking. It lists a phone number that I know off by heart, but I have never been brave enough to ring. She does both in-calls and out-calls. I had to look online to see what these were. It's a lot more expensive for an out-call, which goes hand in hand with the heightened risk on her part, I guess. But her prices are still very reasonable. She sells herself very short if you ask me.

What I like is she really does look like her pictures. A lot of the girls don't. They all tend to use a cocktail of flattering angles, filters, old photos or sometimes just pictures of someone else altogether, which is fraud if you think about it or should at least fall foul of the trade descriptions act. Another thing about her pictures I like is that she doesn't hide her face like a lot of the other girls do. Their faces are pixelated or have black bars over their eyes that remind me of the magazines dad used to hide in his wardrobe.

I remember Mother's self-righteous disgust when we found them after he had gone as if she had never seen them before. As if I hadn't seen them before. As if I hadn't already seen her in their pages. As if I wouldn't have recognised my own bedroom in the photographs in the old biscuit tin hidden in the back of her dresser where she keeps her vibrators.

Her profile, like all the other girls, lists her preferences. Her likes and dislikes. The lines she is willing to cross for a certain amount of money and then the absolute taboo ones that she says she would never do despite graphic video evidence to the contrary. She says she does watersports, both giving and receiving. You have to give her advance notice for these services. I imagine this is so she can have a drink beforehand. Receiving is an extra cost and both are only available as an out-call. I have no real interest in that side of things of course. I'm not a pervert.

She lists BDSM as an interest but only giving, not receiving. Once I had learnt what it meant I found this somewhat frustrating as I'd very much like to tie her down and keep her still for a while. But no means no. I'm very firm on that. So, I'm going to have to think of another way of getting her to listen to me. The rest of her preferences are all very run of the mill, anal at her discretion, oral without protection at her discretion, cum in mouth at her discretion, french-kissing at her discretion and it carries on and on and on and on and all it ever makes me think about is how disgusting you would have to be for her to say no? How dirty would someone's dick have to be for her to not put it in her mouth when I have seen her go straight from ass to mouth with more than a dozen different people? Thankfully the one thing that she very much likes, and is open to everyone, is receiving oral.

I may not be the world's most experienced lover but I'm not entirely naive either. My days at uni were quite tame compared to a lot of people, but being away from home allowed me to explore and experiment a little. Of course, I had to bury that side of me again when I dropped out and returned home but it's still there and I'll always have my memories. The good ones and the bad ones. Foreplay is very important. Dad taught me that, if nothing else. I view it on the same level as vehicle maintenance. You wouldn't drive your car with no oil in it. An engine needs adequate lubrication to run properly. A vagina is exactly the same if you ask me.

THREE

"You'll never guess what I heard Karen telling Courtney that Jess had told Susan but not to tell anyone? You know Jess, the young girl who started as an apprentice in billing? Pretty young thing? Her brother Mike was trying to join the police but got caught dealing before he even took the medical. None of them are very bright to be honest. Their uncle Rory was the one who made the papers when he got himself blowed up in Iraq, or Iran, or Afghanistan or Bosnia, one of those Godless countries we have had to go and put right again anyway. Anyway Karen was telling Courtney, Courtney off reception Courtney not despatch Courtney. Karen was telling Courtney that Jess had told Susan, picking Susan, you know Susan, worked there longer than anyone and is still on the floor? Jess had told Susan that Kerry in IT has only gone and shacked up

with the foreign fella who owns the chippy up by the school. Poor Ryan's body is still warm and she's gone and done that to him. She should be fucking ashamed of herself, the brazen hussy."

They warned me it would hurt. They told me over and over and over. They explained all the procedures and the recovery periods time and time again. And yet I still wasn't prepared for this. It's like my head is being squashed in a vice and pulled apart at the same time. I clench my fists and dig my nails into the palms of my hand just to try and distract myself momentarily.

The pain relief they keep pumping into me gives me these brief glimpses of tranquility. These moments of bliss are then torn away when the pain comes charging back again, seemingly worse than it was before. I can't focus on anything for more than a few seconds. Everything is too loud, too bright, too sharp, too hot, too cold. I want to curl into a ball and scream but everything hurts. Everything hurts. Even thinking hurts. I lick my lips and taste blood.

"I know it's right by the school but it's always full of kids. Always. I'm not saying he's a fiddler or anything like that but why would a grown man open a shop like that right by a school? It's not right. It's creepy if you ask me. It's no wonder kids are so fat these days, would it hurt for him to sell a

salad? He'd probably even get that order wrong, the useless prat. He was meant to be poor Ryan's friend as well. Well if that's how he treats his friends I'd hate to have him as an enemy, that's for certain. And she's been off for months as well. I know she lost her husband, if they were even really married. I don't know anyone who got an invite to that sham. It was probably some hippy dippy hand tying ceremony that isn't even really real, well not in the eyes of the lord."

Her voice is like a drill piercing my soul. Gouging away at my very being. It's so shrill and unrelenting that it's almost enough to take my mind off the pain. Almost. She comes every day without fail. And I know I should be grateful. I know it's not easy as she has to catch two buses. I know she has to catch two buses as it's always the first thing she mentions when she arrives. No "hello" or "how are you doing today?" It's just straight into whatever indignity she has witnessed on the 49 on the way in. I do kind of, almost, feel for her. The public part of public transport is primarily made up of unhygienic imbeciles. But at the same time, I like that she is so bitterly unhappy. It really is what she deserves. Taking into account the weeks I have spent here already, I have around five months of paid sick leave left to use before I even need to think about starting to use my holiday allowance or going back to work. I plan on using every single last day of it just so she has to catch the bus to work, to town, to the doctors, to anywhere and everywhere she needs to go. I've decided that my new purpose in life is to make as many people suffer in any way, shape or form I can possibly manage. No matter how petty. Starting with her.

I think about how easy it would be to replace her lunchbox with a nail bomb and wave her off to work one morning. The hardest part would be getting the timing right. You would want it, you would need it, to go off during rush hour in the centre of town. That's the way to ensure the most casualties. That's the way to ensure the most panic. I think about how easy it would be to paint her out to be some lone wolf type of maniac. Sow the right seeds. Whisper in the right ear. Get her on some government list of potential threats and everyone's a winner.

She's here to see Jenny, the consultant, with me. The idea is that she is here as some type of emotional support, but really, she's just here to get even more dirt to dish on me at work. I try not to think about the things she will have said about me. About the things that happened that night. I can't decide what will be worse, the true things or the fabrications of her diseased mind.

Jenny is here to see how I am

healing and how soon she can get me out of the door. She doesn't say they need the bed but it's clearly high on the agenda. I'm on semi solid food, lots of mashed potato and soup, and that is apparently great progress. I try to tell her that it still feels like my jaw is going to fall off but she just smiles and says that I still need to be careful and patient when it comes to movement for a while. She cheerily says that the swelling is reducing nicely but then adds that we won't know how bad the scarring is until it has gone completely. Her parting shot is that I should be able to speak normally again sometime soon. I don't know if this is her giving me hope and leaving on a high or giving me all the good news first so the bad news at the end doesn't seem so bad. I would ask how long "sometime soon" is but it's not like she'd begin to understand my worries. Despite the pleasantly soothing thoughts of breaking her hands with a clawhammer circling my mind, I smile back at her and the pain that shoots through my skull makes me want to vomit. As soon as Jenny leaves us Mother starts drilling into my brain again.

"They must just let anyone become a doctor these days. I remember when titles were earned, actually meant something and were worthy of respect. She's hardly out of nappies and walking around like her shit doesn't stink? The

fucking nerve of the girl. I bet she only got the job because she's foreign and a woman as well. I mean if you say you're going to see a doctor you just think of a man don't you? I know that probably makes me a racist. After all you're not even allowed to have opinions anymore in case it upsets some stupid snowflake liberal looney leftie student who has no idea about how the world really works. Everyone is too educated these days if you ask me. They all think that just because they have some letters after their names that they know more than ordinary people like me. Well you can't learn everything at university, can you? Let's see how far they make it in this world. I'm surprised she isn't a disabled lesbian to tick all the equality boxes, can't go having a nice normal straight white male having a job now can we? Not while we can import some snotty fucking frog. Still she might well be a lesbian, a lot of people are these days aren't they? She's probably not even a proper lesbian, she's more than likely one of those trendy bisexuals. There was none of that type of behaviour when I was her age and if there was they knew their place and kept quiet about it. Always shoving it in everyone's faces aren't they? With their marches as if that filth is anything to be proud of. It's all political correctness gone mad if you ask me."

I think about how easy it would be to

get a gun. I know I don't know anyone who could get me one straight away but I'm fairly confident I know someone who could ask someone to ask someone. It would just be a case of finding the right starting point without getting too much of the wrong attention. I wonder if it is really like in the movies. If the bang is really that loud. If you really do get the lick of flame from the barrel. I think about pressing the muzzle into her forehead and looking her in the eyes while I pull the trigger. I think about the back of her head painting the wall. I lick my lips and taste blood.

I couldn't sleep so I went for a walk to try and clear my head. It looked like they were harassing someone, so I went over and tried to help. If you pushed me for an explanation as to what happened, that's what I'd tell you. It's what I eventually told the police. It's what was printed in the papers. It sounds reasonable. Believable even. Obviously, it's a lie. I mean of course it's a lie. All the best sounding things in life are lies. The hot singles in your area aren't real. Those pills aren't going to make your dick bigger. There are no Nigerian princes looking to offload millions of dollars. That dog you loved with all of your heart as a child didn't go to live on a farm, your dad killed it with a spade then buried it in the garden when you were at school.

So, what did kick it all off? It wasn't self defence on their part, I wasn't armed. I posed no real threat to anyone. They certainly weren't harassing her; they weren't even near her when I first got there. They weren't some hoodie wearing gang looking for trouble. They were just four normal guys looking for a bit of fun on a friday night.

The girls call them punters or Johns. There is a whole new language of slang you will need to learn if that is the life you want to lead. You have to know all the right things to say and when to say them if you don't want to look like some naive little idiot looking to get robbed or worse still an undercover copper.

They were Johns looking for a bit of action after a night out. A bit of harmless fun that their wives or girlfriends or mothers never need to know about. Why were they there? Maybe they have a little quirk their partner isn't down with and this is their release. Maybe they aren't getting any at home. Maybe they have no partner, and the girls are better than a hand-job in front of the laptop. Maybe they just like the seedy thrill of it all. Who knows? Who cares? It's not important. They were there. Wrong place, wrong time. But why did they do what they did to me? What drove these men to beat me half to death? There really is only one answer and it's hilariously simple. I was asking for it.

FOUR

"So, I heard David was telling Angela how Darren, Gough, not Pugh or Carlisle, has only gone and miscounted an entire container. I don't know if it was up or down, but it all had to be recalled, repacked and then recounted. They didn't even pull him up on it! Of course, we got some nice overtime out of it but that's besides the point isn't it? What if I had plans? They never think about things like that do they? And he's still walking around like he's cock of the fucking walk when he can't even tally a manifest correctly. I've never liked him. I told Susan as soon as he walked in he was clearly an idiot. First impressions are never wrong and I've never met a Darren yet who isn't some type of retard. Carlisle is just as bad, if not worse, but he gets it off his mum. Spazzy Spencer was what we used to call her at school, that was her maiden

name, not that you're allowed to call people spastics anymore of course. If Rory Carlisle and Spazzy Spencer got together now they'd call it grooming and put him on some type of register the dirty bastard. Three years older than her he was. We were in fifth form and he was in college. We met him on an open day, he was our groups chaperone. Showing us around the campus telling us where things were acting all nicey nicey. At the end of the day I asked him if he was going to ask me out and he said he preferred her. Her?! Spazzy Spencer? Tells you everything about the man if you ask me."

Two weeks I lasted on the sick. Two weeks. Two days. Two whole fucking days at home was all I managed to get her to still catch the bus to and from work. Really it was all my own fault it fell apart. Just like it always is. She asked me on the second morning what I was doing up and about and I said I was going to go into town to pick up my prescriptions and get the papers. She said she'd get a lift in with me as I was heading that way anyway and then it was just assumed I'd pick her up after work and then do it the next day and the next day and the next day. My life is stuck in this mundane nightmare loop and I'm the only one who can break it.

The doctor asked me if I was sure I wanted to go back to work. I made up some bullshit excuse about needing to keep busy and wanting to get back to getting on with my life. They asked if I was in any pain and I told them I hardly even notice it anymore while gritting my new teeth and squinting so I could see her through the agony. She either didn't notice or care and carried on with her tick sheet of questions to determine if I was fit to work or not. The thing about doctors is as long as you know what to say and when to say it you can get whatever you want out of them. Same as most people really.

Work took a different approach. On the face of it, it looked like they had my best interests at heart. They asked all the right questions, am I sure I want to come back already? Do I want to go on light duties or a phased return? They assured me that no one would think any less of me if I chose to take it a bit easy for a while before then asking if I could work at the weekend. No pressure, obviously, all overtime is entirely voluntary, but it's just that they do have a backlog of containers that need to be double checked and they have the big end of year audit coming up.

In their defence, they didn't put me straight back on the shop floor. I don't know if they were trying to protect me or my colleagues. Normally people on phased returns end up on the front desk. It's like they think the shame of answering the phones and greeting customers and suppliers makes people want to get back to their normal role that little bit faster. But there were no reception duties for me. I'm different. I'm special. I'm sure it had nothing to do with the fact that I look like something out of a horror movie. And it definitely had nothing to do with the way my jaw constantly clicks and locks making me fairly incoherent. After all that would be discrimination wouldn't it? And we can't have that in this day and age. It's political correctness gone mad.

So, I find myself on QC, quality control, it's a fairly new role and I'm told if I can prove myself I'm in with a shout for it full time, if I want it of course. They don't bully people into or out of roles anymore. Not after what happened to poor Ryan. All I have to do is check the packer's trollies to make sure they match the manifest. No one in management openly says this is all down to Darren and his errant counting but it quite clearly is.

The rest of the girls on the floor don't see it that way of course. They all see it as an attack on their work. And it kind of is, sure Darren messed his count up but none of them pointed this out to him or anyone else. They all just stood there and bundled up whatever landed in front of them and never said a word as it was loaded onto the wagon. Would I have done anything differently if I was there? Probably not. Would I say if something was so clearly wrong now I've got a clipboard and a pen on a bit of string? Probably not. See the thing is I really don't care about any of this. Any of them. Any of you. None of this is important in the grand scheme of things. But then again very little is, is it?

I can't shake the feeling that she is important. Maybe not on a global scale. I'm sure she doesn't hold the secrets to world peace. She won't know how to save the whales or stop the ice caps melting. But she just might be able to make me not feel so alone while we are all drowning.

I kind of hoped she would come and visit me in the hospital. Really, it's the only reason I agreed to the interviews and pictures. I'm not saying I was trying to pull on her heart strings, but if you saw someone beaten half to death in front of you and then saw them in the papers alongside an appeal for witnesses, surely you'd do something wouldn't you? I know I probably would. Well it depends on who it was and what they did to deserve the beating, I guess. Or who dished the beating out, that's got to be a factor as well hasn't it? Maybe she doesn't read the papers? Not everyone does anymore do they? It's only something I do as it was a habit dad instilled in me from a young age. I tried getting him to read it all online, but he insisted that print was the one true medium and that we'd all miss it once it was gone. The thing is I don't think we will. If anything, the sooner their power is wrested from their hands the better. It's not news, not really, not anymore. It's just the opinions of billionaires drip fed into the ears of the common man. The world that they portray isn't really real. Or at least it isn't as bad as they make out. If half the shit they say is happening or, is going to happen happened, none of us would leave the house in the morning. I remember when it was AIDS that was going to kill us all, then it was cancer, then Ebola, then cancer again and yet we are all still here. I dare you to watch the news and then look out of your window and compare the two. Sometimes all you can trust is what is right in front of you.

She doesn't read the papers and she doesn't really like what she does for a living. I know that much for sure now and I almost know her name, I think. What I need to do is try and put an accurate age to her so I can piece together who she really is. To find out if she is who I need her to be.

The main problem with porn, or at least mainstream professional porn, is anyone up to their mid twenties is classed as being a teen and then anything over somehow classes you as a milf. There is no middle ground. You're either barely legal or over the hill. Then you have the gilf, a tiny field of whores who either genuinely like what they do or are in too deep to get out.

Darcy is well out of her teens, but she isn't quite a gilf yet. She isn't as agile as she used to be but if you can get past the fear there is still life in her eyes. For now, anyway.

"You know me, I'm not one to spread gossip for the sake of it but I think it's only right you know what the other girls are saying. Ellie told me that Chantel had heard Maisy say to Carrie that she thinks you've got it in for us all. I told her that Carrie doesn't know anything about anything but that's what they are saying. I told them just because you keep pulling them up on honest silly little mistakes doesn't mean it's anything personal against them. It isn't, is it? You do know that any one of us could walk round with that clipboard and do whatever it is you think that you're doing. You're not different. You're not special. You watch, as soon as your phased return is over and done with you'll be back down on the floor with us and then we'll soon see how accurate your trollies are won't we? Honestly if your father could see you strutting around he'd be fucking ashamed of you. No one, and I mean no one, likes a grass. Remember that. There is only so much protection I can give you. It's not like I haven't put my neck on the line for you is it? Remember it was me that got you the job in the first place and this is how you repay me?"

I try to not pay attention. I try to focus on the seemingly infinite stream of brake lights in front of us. I try and melt into the pain behind my eyes. I grit my teeth until something new cracks inside my head and grip the steering wheel with every bit of strength I can muster and all I can think of is how much I need to get hold of a gun. I lick my lips and taste blood.

Despite the atmosphere in the car, despite the rain and how we worked over and the fact I need to get home because I'm long overdue some painkillers, Mother still insists on going to see dad on the way home. I hate that she calls it going to see him, as if he is in the hospital, or in respite, or in a home. As if he is ever coming back.

She likes to go in the afternoon. It's generally busier then so there is more chance people will see her playing the role of faithful, poor, tragic, grieving, widow. She never leaves flowers. She never says anything, or at least nothing out loud any way. She just sits there looking around waiting to be seen for a few minutes then sighs and leaves. I like to go on my own, either very late at night or very early in the morning so I have the place to myself. It's just me and dad, the way it used to be. There is something soothing about the silence of a graveyard, especially when you can hear your piss splashing on the headstone.

FIVE

"Sian is the one you need to be keeping an eye on if you ask me. Nothing but trouble that one. Never stops talking, always running her gums. And none of it is ever about anything of any substance, all of it is just idle gossip. I don't even know where she gets most of it from, the nosey little cow. She's never got nothing good to say about anyone as well, you spend ten minutes in the fag shelter with her and there isn't a person in the building she wouldn't stab in the back. Nice as fucking pie to their face of course, the two-faced little madam. I heard her yesterday slagging off Linzie from HR because she wouldn't tell her why Jake and Cath had both been marched off the premises. I know it's because they were caught at it in the back of the stores but seeing as she never asked me if I knew anything I didn't tell her, and it's none of her

fucking business anyway I've always known they were at it, both of them married as well the dirty bastards. Still you can't really blame Cath for looking elsewhere given the state of Barry these days. No one has even seen him in years, not properly anyway. He was always a bit batty but he tried his best. I mean he had a job and was always clean and tidy but after the court case he just crumbled into dust. I know they found him innocent in the end but there is no smoke without fire if you ask me and that poor girl was only just sixteen after all. And as for Jake he'd put his dick in a drainpipe if he thought it would get him off. The things I have heard about him would make a whore blush."

Jake, who is gay, and Cath actually got sacked and then escorted from the premises because they were stealing items from stock and selling them online. I know this because it was me who found the shortage of items in their trolleys and then matched it with the discrepancies with the stock in the stores. It was me who then found the exact same items for sale online. It was me who alerted their respective bosses to what was going on. I've not told Mother any of this as she never asked me if I knew anything and it's none of her business anyway. Management is really pleased with the work I have been doing, mispicks and short shipments have reduced greatly, I've already caught two thieves and everyone is a little bit wary of being under constant scrutiny so are being more diligent. I could tell you that I don't enjoy the power that I've been given but that would be a lie. I love it and I'm only getting started. I want them to fear me. I want everyone to fear me.

"Of course you wouldn't know anything about Jake and Cath though would you now? Would you? I mean you're not that much of a cowardly arsehole are you? You wouldn't do the dirty on your friends, your colleagues, like that and then try and hide it. Would you?"

The insinuation and spite dripping from every word is almost impressive. In the past I would have been scared and confessed everything, but she genuinely doesn't know what I have done. There is no way she can find out either, she doesn't know I'm now authorised to not only go into the stores, but can check their work as well. The pickers think I'm checking the packers work. The packers think I'm checking the pickers work. I'm not sure what the stores think I'm up to, but it doesn't matter, I answer to none of them. None of them answer to me. I am an unstoppable force of nature, an agent of chaos. I am godlike.

"If I do find out you have had anything

to do with this, anything at all, I'll let everyone know what a two-faced piece of shit you really are. I'll not hold anything back. At all. Every little shitty thing you ever did as a kid, that time you pissed yourself on the playground because you were too shy to ask the teacher if you could go to the toilet. All the times you came crying to us in the night because you were afraid someone was coming for you. Everyone will know just how fucking pathetic you really are. I'll make you wish you'd never been fucking born let alone survived whatever nonsense it was that you were up to that night."

I honestly can't decide if she really suspects that I have had a hand in their demise or if she is just angry and lashing out at the nearest target. Either way I say nothing to her as I know that'll make her angrier than any defence or denial ever could.

"Everyone knows what goes on in that part of town. Everyone. They are saying you were out there trying to sell yourself. As if anyone would have paid to have a go on you. And what am I meant to tell them? That you weren't? That just opens up the possibility that you were there to pay for it. I honestly can't decide what is the worst option there. Either way you disgust me to my very core. I can hardly bring myself to look at you, let alone speak to you. I'm

just glad your father isn't here to have to go through this, it would have finished him off for sure."

Well that confirms it for sure. She knows nothing. She's desperate. Her last line of attack is always to bring him up. It used to be the same when I was a kid, and he was still alive. She used to dish out the "Wait until your father hears about this" line a lot when I was a kid as if he was ever anything to fear. Then after he died, he became a different sort of weapon to wield. The shame that he never had in life became magnified tenfold. My actions, no matter how big or small, were an embarrassment or a slight to his memory, to his legacy. As if either are worth anything anyway. It's not like she even held him in high regard when he was around. She literally cuckolded him, belittled him, used him in the same way she uses everyone. She likes to tell people how it was her that found him. How she rang for the ambulance and, with the help of the responder on the phone, tried to bring him back until they arrived. She likes to paint this picture of herself as this tragic hero who tried her best, but sadly failed. She tells people he was still warm when she found him and then curses her luck that she wasn't just five minutes earlier.

I never meant to kill him, well that's not quite true. I never set out to kill him on that day and in that manner. It wasn't a planned act of patricide, well not fully. I had wanted to kill him, to kill someone, anyone, for a long while, so when the opportunity arose, I took it. He'd not been well for as long as anyone cares to remember but towards the end, he was bed bound, pissing in a bag and struggling to breath on his own. The hospice set him up with an oxygen mask and enough pain relief to make sure all he really did was sleep. Honestly, it was an act of mercy. I should be able to tell people what I did and have them thank me. Instead the hole in the hose was put down to a kink getting caught on the corner of the bed and wearing itself thin. An accident. A sad tragic accident that no one could have foreseen.

He took a while to die and it didn't look like fun. His eyes bulging, wide with panic, as each time he tried to take a breath, nothing happened. It got a bit boring after the first five minutes or so, so I went and got a bag of crisps from the kitchen. I asked if he wanted anything before I left him, I'm not a monster. He was still there, gasping away like a landed carp when I got back. I was thankful for that as I'd never have forgiven myself for missing his last breath. I wanted to know what that tastes like. I needed to look into someone's eyes as the lights went out. He hung around long enough for me to finish my crisps, which I thought was pretty decent of him.

When his breathing became ragged and shallower with every effort, I leant over him as if I was going to kiss him and inhaled his last breath. I think I was trying to capture whatever was left of his being as it departed his mortal body. As his eyes fluttered closed and death rattled out of him, I whispered into his ear "Looks like I fucked you for once doesn't it?"

I stood and watched him for a while to make sure he had gone and definitely wasn't coming back. All the while holding my breath, holding his breath. Savouring the silence and enjoying the serenity that had washed over me. Mother was working over and was due home any minute, so I dragged myself away from him and left through the back yard, grabbing another packet of crisps on my way through the kitchen. I looped through the park a few times, threw stones at the stupid ducks for a bit, called at the offie and bought a very nice bottle of Malbec and then went back home. Mother was already in full blown widow mode by the time I got there. The ambulance was still sitting on the drive. The paramedics had long stopped trying to revive dad and were focusing all of their soothing skills onto her. Even his last day on earth ended up being about her. I kind of liked that to be honest.

Just thinking, fleetingly, about his final moments is almost enough to drown

Mother and all of her venom out. It's even almost enough to make me forget about the pain behind my eyes that is constantly threatening to drive me insane. That day is something I try not to think about too much as I never want it to lose its vitality. The memory alone is almost enough to get me through those difficult days. If I think hard enough about how sweet his breath tasted, I don't want to hurt anyone anymore. I don't hurt anymore. But the more she goes on and on and on and on the harder and harder it gets. Unless I can find some other way to make her shut up and leave me alone. I'm going to have to help her along the way to meet dad. I bite my tongue trying not to giggle at the thought of the light leaving her eyes. I lick my lips and taste blood.

SIX

"Jane, Jones not Skyrme, reckons that Jake was only bloody dealing drugs and has gone and got Cath hooked on the old wacky backy. This is why she's been so spaced out and next to fucking useless these past few months. So sacking Jake is fair enough if you ask me but poor Cath is a victim here. I might point this out to Alex the union rep, mind you he isn't worth a pot of piss is he?"

Mother used to accuse me of being on drugs, it was her go to for a very long time. She always said it explained the way I was. Quiet. Withdrawn. Antisocial. She never, ever thought that maybe her overbearing presence, her desire for absolute control over my life had anything to do with me not wanting to say much. Or that I didn't do a lot because anything I did do was somehow wrong in her eyes. In the end she took me to the doctors and demanded they do blood tests. I went along with it because I wanted to see her face when they came back clean. She just said that it didn't prove anything and that doctors got stuff wrong all the time.

"Jane is one to talk though, her eldest boy, Brian, is a dirty junkie. Gavin, Wilson not Ince, caught him, needle in hand in the toilets of the White Lion months ago. Didn't even try and deny it when Gavin took the needle off him and smashed it. The withdrawal got so bad he ended up in hospital for a while. And Rigsby still didn't bar him! Tells you everything about the state of the place if you ask me."

Brian is a diabetic. Gavin is a vile piece of shit who knew exactly what he was doing when he took Brian's insulin off him. She is right though the White Lion is a bit of a shit hole. It is the place to go if you want to buy stolen goods, drugs or just socialise with the dregs of humanity. Rigsby turns a blind eye to the odd deal here and there because he sells duty free fags from behind the bar. The way he looks at it is he won't grass on you if you don't grass on him. Says it all if you ask me.

"I remember when all the pubs in town used to be decent. There were ones you wouldn't go in, of course, The Rainbow Club was for the Labour voting rabble,

everyone drinking on a tab, it's no wonder the place went belly up in the end. The Vic was full of the real ale crowd, all pipe smoke and tedious talk about hoppy mouthfeels and other such nonsense. The Crown was our favourite of course, wasn't our local, that was The Tavern on the Hill but was full of dole bludgers pissing the family allowance away. The Crown was just lovely, well worth the walk into town if you ask me. Neil the landlord got that Thai lad in, Keung or some such gobbledygook. We all just called him Bruce. He ended up answering to it in the end. They put on some of the best food around. Of course he couldn't cook a Sunday roast to save his life so if you were after food on a Sunday you always went to the Travelers, but you had to book your table in advance or sit and wait on the off chance they could squeeze you in."

It's at times like this that I ask myself if anyone would miss her if I just caved her head in and dumped her in the canal. She adds nothing to anyone's life. I would be doing a public service really. I would deserve a medal and the freedom of the town, maybe they could even make me mayor. Is that how you become mayor? Not by killing someone I mean but earning it by being an upstanding citizen. I think I'd make a good mayor, not like it's a hard job is it? Drive round in a Jag, cut a few ribbons, open the new supermarket, judge the beautiful babies competition at the show. Plus, you get to wear those cool gold chains, don't you?

"You're not even fucking listening to me are you? Look at you away on cloud cuckoo land again. I'll tell you something if you're on the drugs again you can get out of this house once and for all. I'd rather be on my own than have to worry about living with a junkie. Having to hide all my jewelry, taking my purse to bed at night with me. Locking my bedroom door. I won't do it, so you better sort you act out or you'll be out on what's left of your ear."

She's right, I wasn't listening to her, but I can tell you that I know I wasn't missing out on anything earth shattering. She hadn't figured out how to cure cancer or end global hunger. And she definitely wasn't going to tell me about how Kirsty is pregnant and that the father isn't her loving faithful husband Marc, it's actually Oskar the Polish lorry driver, who she screwed at the Summer Ball. I'm not sure if anyone else knows that yet, mind. I'd quite like to tell her, just to see her reaction. That might be the snippet of information I give to her just before I kill her. I don't know when and I don't know how but I do know I need her gone. I can't cope with this anymore. She is just a blight.

I was on my way home from the ball that night. I hadn't actually gone. I didn't have a ticket. No one had asked me if I wanted to go. Everyone just assumed, correctly, that I wanted no part of it. But then the night came around and Mother had her gown on and yeah, she looked good and I was a bit jealous. I thought about going and trying to blag my way in. I thought about saying that I had lost my ticket. I thought about going, blocking the exits, and burning the place down. I thought about a lot of things that night and only acted on one of them.

Everyone looked so beautiful and happy and relaxed. They all looked so comfortable in their own skins. I wanted to know what that felt like, so I went looking for her. I went looking for them. The ball was at the golf course, the posh one, The Lodges, not the one on the edge of town that lets just anyone rock up and play. I gave Mother and Simon, her date for the evening, a lift in. They were both very adamant about not needing one back and I knew then that he was fucking her. Not that it matters, they are both single and I thought that maybe if she found someone new, she'd leave me alone for a bit. So, I gave them a lift and then I just sort of didn't leave right away.

I watched the night unfold from the darkness of the greens. I saw Kirsty and Oskar sneak out, hand in hand, giggling and all over each other before they went into the bushes. I watched them all dance and drink and eat and laugh and I had never felt so alone in my life. I stayed and watched the night unfold until the groundsman came out to get the fireworks ready for the big finale and then I left. I drove home with the intention of just going to bed. Going to sleep and putting it all behind me in the same way I do with everything else on every other day of my life. But I couldn't sleep. I didn't want to sleep. I wanted to feel loved and needed and wanted. I wanted to be happy. I wanted to belong. So I got back up and went for a walk.

I walked because I didn't want the car being caught on camera and then traced back to me. I walked because I didn't want to get caught kerb-crawling like one of those pathetic, sad wanker Johns. I walked because I guess I knew, deep down, I wouldn't be coming back one way or another.

Her overnight fees are very reasonable compared to the other girls. She only asks for £700, some of the others charge over a thousand pounds. I withdrew the full £300 my bank allows me from the cashpoint outside the old market and reasoned that as it was so late it would probably be enough. I mean I wasn't asking for a full night, was I? It was already past midnight. Meaning that technically it was morning, and I should have been paying her hourly £100 in-call fee. Three hours would have been more than enough time for what I needed from her.

She was leant against a streetlight, bathed in orange and blowing cigarette smoke up into the night sky. I wish she didn't smoke, it's the one and only thing I can fault her on. If you look close enough at her pictures you can see the wrinkles around her mouth from years of sucking down that filth. I know her profile says she is always showered and minty fresh, but that stench never fully goes away does it? It's always there clinging to your clothes or your hair. Even chewing gum doesn't mask it fully.

She looked so beautiful under the light, like something out of an old noir film. I wanted her to see how beautiful she was, so I took a picture of her and that's when things started to go wrong.

I hadn't heard her speak before. Not properly anyway. The thing she says in her videos don't count. They can't count. Not really. Her begging to be fucked or saying how much she likes whatever they are doing to her are a world away from the abuse she started to hurl at me. She was shouting for help and saying that I was another one of those weirdos, whatever that means.

I didn't even see where the first one came from. What happened was my phone was knocked out of hand and then kicked away from me. He was pushing and prodding me in the chest asking if I was looking for trouble. I told him I wasn't, and I really wasn't, but he either didn't hear or believe me, and out of the two of us it was him who was looking for trouble if you ask me.

The next two got out of a car together and I sort of hoped they were undercover police, or at least concerned citizens, but they joined in with the first fella. The one kept asking what I was and I wasn't sure how to reply so I focused on the other one who was asking if I wanted a good kicking. The fourth and final one came at me from down the alley and was the one who swung the first punch. He was a big lad and put all of his weight behind it. I felt and heard my nose crunch in on itself. I tried to get a handle on what was happening. Tried to focus on one of the voices that were screaming at me. I cleared my throat to try and speak. I licked my lips and tasted blood. I wanted to tell them to leave me alone, but once they started hitting me, they just didn't stop and after a while I didn't want them to.

SEVEN

"You'll never guess what, I only heard Kirsty telling Aishia that her and Marc are expecting. I never thought I'd see the day, they've been married years and he still doesn't look like he's got half a decent fuck in him. Still just because she says they are expecting doesn't mean it's his does it now? Of course there are all sorts of rumours about them and what they get up to. Not that I'm a prude of course but those types of activities have to take a backburner once you get lumbered with kids. No matter how much you miss having anything that resembles a life."

It's not that Mother really resents ever having me, after all she loves to constantly remind me of the hoops they had to jump through to get me. It's more that she actively despises me for not being the status symbol she thought I'd be. As she likes to constantly remind me, I'm nothing but an abject failure, a pathetic loser, a waste of cum. Nothing.

Really it all started in primary school. I was never the lead role of the play or the captain of the team, not that I ever even made the team. I was never the fastest or the brightest. My pictures never went on the fridge. I never got commendations or a Blue Peter badge. I just coasted along, amazingly average at everything that came my way.

If anything, she would have preferred me to be bottom of the class. To be the dumbest, the slowest, the last picked for all the playground games. I would still have been a burden but at least then I would have had the decency to make her a martyr while doing it. She tried, of course she tried. There were the tests for ADD, ADHD, dyslexia, autism, dyspraxia, the never ending, eternally humiliating search for an explanation as to why I was the way I was. Why I am the way I am. It's hard to strive and achieve when all you've ever been told is how much of a disappointment to everyone you are.

"Still when Kirsty swans off on maternity at least you'll have to come back into the real world and do some actual work instead of walking round like your shit doesn't stink. The girls are talking about refusing to do anymore overtime until you are stopped going over everything with a fine-tooth comb.

Did you know that Nita found poor Rachel, Stanners not Miller, crying in the toilets the other day? Who cares if she accidently put in an extra bundle? Shit happens. The customer isn't going to complain so don't give me that shit again and we made how many million in profits last year? It's not like it's a big deal. Kelvin is still going to get his new car at the end of the year, isn't he?"

Kelvin getting a new car is something that has been bandied about for even longer than I've worked here. It all goes back to the year of the merger with Cravens. The business didn't technically make a profit so no performance bonuses were paid out, but Kelvin had a new company car. He'll be the first to tell you that it may have looked bad, but his old car was out of contract and it was actually cheaper in the long run to have a new one. But no one ever cares about the facts of stories like this do they? Why look at things objectively when you could just get angry and lash out instead?

"Of course your father never liked Kelvin. He always knew a bullshitter when he saw one and was never afraid to speak up for everyone. They went to school together as well. He might talk like he's got a plum in his mouth these days, but let me tell you something Mr High-and-fucking-mighty grew up down on

the Moors with the rest of the filth, his mother was a dirty fucking slattern as well."

Darcy lives down on the Moors, or at least that is where the house that she takes in-calls is anyway. I can't see her earning enough to be able to keep two houses on the go. She isn't that popular outside of town's sordid little bubble. Her videos never win any awards. She does go on tours every so often. She'll advertise that she is going to be in London, Cardiff, Birmingham, Manchester, Stoke, Dundee, Carlisle, anywhere that has a place where hope goes to die. She always says that she is looking forward to seeing you all again. I dream of going to these places and rescuing her from whatever ordeals she is put through in the cheap hotel rooms you see in the photos. They all have the same stained carpets and dirty linen. Pedal bins full of used rubbers. She is always smiling but it never reaches her eyes.

I have never been able to figure out if her going on tour, and the Johns going to the hotel to see her, counts as an in-call or out-call. I do know that the tours always mean she takes more group bookings. Gangs of potbellied, middle-aged men. All blurred out tattoos and very visible wedding rings. How do you end up in a room like that? How do you make friends like that? Are there group messages sent round asking who is free next Thursday night and fancies going shares on a whore? Do they get a minibus, or all arrive separately? How do they decide who gets to go first? Who gets to go last? Do they draw straws or is there a clear hierarchy? Her world, her life is so alien to me. It doesn't disgust me, not really anyway. I just think she deserves better and if I have to pay for her company to tell her so then so be it.

That was the plan that night. I just wanted to talk to her. Tell her that I love her and that I am there for her. I still am as well, even after all the unpleasantness. See, she's broken like me. She might put on a brave face, but her scars are there for all to see. Before the attack all of my scars were on the inside. At least now the outside matches. It's important to look for the positives, that's what the doctors used to say. Dad used to say I wasn't wired right. Mother says I'm damaged goods. They both told me how they would have sent me back if they could. They used to joke about how they weren't given a receipt when they picked me up.

I'm going to do it properly this time. I'm going to save up my wages, get a room for the night at The Oak. One of the nice ones, maybe the Honeymoon Suite, and hire her for the night. I know she has worked from there before as I've seen the pictures online, so she'll feel safe. I'll even use a fake name, so

she won't refuse the booking or not turn
up.

I'll make out like I'm new in town
or on business and just looking for
company for the evening. I'll say I'm
going to take her out for a nice meal,
treat her all special then take her back
to the room on the premise of
conventional, normal intercourse. I
won't tell her I just want to talk to
her for a bit, or that I know who she
really is. I'll pretend I am just
another grubby nobody looking to use her
body. I think she'll like that.

But first I need to deal with
Mother. I would tell you that I'm not
looking forward to it, but that would be
a lie. I think about the light leaving
her eyes. I clench my teeth to stop
myself moaning in ecstasy. Something
chips off at the back of my mouth and I
run my tongue over it until it's swollen
and sore. I lick my lips and taste
blood.

I have stopped taking the
painkillers. They barely touched the
incessant throbbing in my brain and
never even slowed the grinding of the
bones of my skull. I still collect the
prescriptions as regular as clockwork. I
still go to the doctors and put on a
brave face and convince them I still
need them while saying that I don't. I
still feel like my head is going to
explode at any minute. By this point I
have quite a few stashed away, more than
enough for a dozen overdoses if you can

ever believe what you read online.

I've started grinding them down and adding them to Mother's food and drink. Gradually getting her hooked without even realising it. I know they are working when she starts to slur her words and nods off. If I can keep this up one day soon, she'll go to sleep and then just never wake up.

I've dreamt about Darcy from the very first time I set eyes on her. I was fifteen and had bunked off school. Mother was at work and dad was meant to have been as well. I wasn't a prolific skiver, but I had a free study period after lunch and didn't see the point of going back for the final lesson. It was only German anyway and I was never planning on going anywhere that needed me to sprechen any Deutsch.

I had the place to myself when I first got home so I made myself a sandwich and went to my room to read. That was my idea of the perfect way to spend my free time. To be honest it still sounds pretty good. It's not that I was ever actively discouraged from reading or studying or anything like that but I was told that as I wasn't pretty and didn't have tits I'd have to find some other way to attract boys and that no one liked a smart ass.

When I heard the door, I assumed I had nodded off for a while as I should have had the place to myself until gone five. I knew something was amiss when my name wasn't called out straight away. I always had to have the tea on by the time they got home and the days I forgot, I was reminded how useless I am before they even set eyes on me. No excuse was ever good enough no matter how true or false they were.

He obviously assumed he had the place to himself as well as they headed straight up the stairs and to the marital bed. At that age I already knew that being with Mother wasn't good for your confidence and for the next hour all he seemed to do was ask her if she liked whatever it was that he was doing to her. I knew she was a liar because she kept telling him yes and no one should like the things he did.

I got my first real look at her as I tried to sneak across the landing. My plan was, I could make it back to school and I wouldn't even be that late for German and just pretend the whole thing had never happened. I was at the top of the stairs when she came out of the bedroom and was heading towards the bathroom. We both stopped and stared, neither of us said a word, time seemed to freeze, and I think we both had the same look of panic and fear in our blue grey eyes. Dad broke the spell by shouting at her to hurry up as he was ready to go again and she needed to be gone before his bitch wife and dumb kid got back.

She looked at me and smiled. It was tender and caring and warm and had genuine affection behind it. She shrugged her shoulders and went to the bathroom. I crept downstairs, knowing which stairs creaked and which ones didn't, I left the house through the back and hid in the park until it was time to go home again.

I lost track of time and got back late. You could always tell when he had got laid. The black clouds would lift, and he'd be like a new man. There he was cooking the tea, whistling along to the radio as if everything was right in the world. He told me Mother was working late and asked where I had been. It wasn't accusingly or angry, he seemed to be genuinely interested for once. I told him I had stayed back a bit as I needed a few tips from my German teacher. Dad told me, cheerily, that learning any language was a waste of time as everyone spoke English and anyone who didn't weren't worth worrying about.

EIGHT

"Angie said, Angie said, Angie? Angela, Angel, Anne, Annnie, Ang, Anna. Was it Anna? Who were we talking about? Is it hot in here or is it just me? Annalise said I looked tired, the fucking nerve of that woman. I don't even know who I think she is. Do you?"

I know I shouldn't gloat but it's really hard not to at times like this. It's the middle of the afternoon and she is wasted. She didn't get out of bed until gone noon, completely missed today's overtime and doesn't even realise it yet. That'll pay off nicely come Monday morning. If she makes it that far.

Mary Anne said that Mother looked tired because I not so subtly pointed it out to her the other day. I was perfectly playing the doting child, making out I was worried about how much she was taking on of late. How the silly little mistakes that people were finally starting to notice were due to her running herself into the ground trying to keep our heads above water. I poured my heart out to her at the coffee machine. I wasn't sure how we were going to make the next mortgage payment. Lie. I wasn't even sure why she had remortgaged the house in the first place. Lie. I hear her up in the middle of the night crying. Lie. I'm worried about this fella she's been talking to online. Lie. I think she might be drinking on the sly. Lie. I'm worried she is going to go the same way as dad did. Lie. I'm not worried about that in the slightest.

We have started having a bottle or two of wine on an evening. The leaflet that comes with my medication that she is on says not to and I was curious as to why. Turns out it's hilarious. She pissed herself the night before last. She came round in the bath as I was washing the sick out of her hair. Before she came back to reality, I was considering drowning her there and then. It would have been easy enough to make it look like an accident. I could have staved her head in on the taps, so it looked like she slipped. I could have lit some candles, left a book and a half empty glass of wine on the side and have it look like she fell asleep while having a nice relaxing soak.

Her eyes cleared and her brain caught up to where she was and what was going on. She started to cry and said that she was sorry. So very, very, sorry. I had never heard those words out of her mouth before and it knocked me. For a brief moment she wasn't this ogre anymore. She was this little old woman, caught in a trap of her own making with no idea of how to get out. Then the real her surfaced again and she snapped at me that I was using the wrong shampoo. The cheap shit in the bathroom is for my mop. She keeps the stuff she gets at the salon in her bedroom away from my grubby paws.

I could have ended it there and then and maybe I should have. Only I kind of don't want to do it in a flash of anger. I don't want to do it on a whim and I certainly don't want to be half drunk when it happens. Instead I smiled my broken smile. The one that almost hides the torment in my eyes and went and got the expensive stuff that I don't deserve to use. The stuff in the red bottle on her dressing table that I occasionally piss in to amuse myself.

Their room was always off limits. Always. I was never allowed in there no matter what. Not when I was little and was sick or had had a nightmare. If I wanted a drink in the night I was to knock on the door and wait for them to answer. They had their room and I had mine and that was that. As I got older and more independent, I found myself wanting to go in there more than ever. I was drawn to it like a moth to a flame.

It started off as quick, stolen, furtive glances. Mother would be in the bath, dad mowing the lawn or whatever and I'd dash in. I think that is where all of my... issues arise from. Those cheap, quick and easy thrills gave me a thirst that I could never quite quench. At first, I used to stand in there and just look around. I didn't even know what I was looking at or for, but I desperately tried to soak up all the information I could in the few seconds I dared to be in there. The more I did it the braver I became. I forced myself to push it that little bit further each time. To stay a scant few seconds longer. Before too long I was spending minutes at a time in there. Rifling through their drawers, their wardrobes, looking under the bed, staring at the ceiling and imagining what it was like to be them.

As I got older and wiser to the world, I grew more horrified and disgusted at the things I saw and found. I eventually realised that the friends who came over on a Friday and Saturday night weren't really my uncles or aunties. That the comments on how much I was growing up weren't innocent and well-meant compliments. I got caught once. Of course, I got caught. Part of me always wanted to get caught. Getting caught was all part of the game they didn't know they were playing until it was too late.

Mother had gone to see Uncle Geoff and Aunty Sue. She was staying overnight like she always did even though they only lived on the other side of town. Dad announced he was going to pop to the offie to get some cans in for the big game even though he despised football and wouldn't really be watching it. He asked me if I wanted to go with him and then if I wanted anything after I said no. As soon as the door closed behind him, I dashed upstairs and treated myself to a luxurious nose around.

Mother had taken her little carry-on case of toys, restraints and outfits with her so there wasn't a lot to delve into but somehow, I still didn't hear him come back. I never heard if he called my name from the foot of the stairs like they always did if they thought I was home before them. The first I knew about his return was him asking what the hell I thought I was doing. The next thing I knew I was face down on their bed. That was the first time he taught me a lesson. That's how he always phrased it. Teaching me a lesson. It was never an act he ever claimed to enjoy or took any pleasure out of. It was always for my own good.I always needed to learn my place. It was always used as a punishment, no matter how small the transgression. The first blow was across my face. An open-handed slap. A seemingly effeminate blow thrown with the full force of an angry grown man. I licked my lips and tasted blood.

After that night they had a lock on their bedroom door and eventually I had one on mine as well. Both of them locked from the outside. Both keeping me out and in simultaneously. I don't know if he ever told her about the things he did to me or if they were just his dirty little secret, but she went along with the games anyway. I still went into their room whenever the chance arose. The desire was still there. The desire is always there. If anything, the harder they fought to keep me out the more I fought to get in. I was never caught again but it somehow didn't matter. The thrill of the chase was illicit and that high is something I'm still chasing.

It was a few months after I was caught, and I became his personal plaything that I first saw her. She was, and still is, the link that connects everything. All I need is some time to explain it all to her. Really, that's what I was trying to do that night. I just wanted to talk to her. Nothing more and nothing less. Things just got a little out of hand as they always do. It wasn't her fault. It was never going to be her fault. She is innocent in all of this. She's the only one who can possibly come out of this well. I wonder if she knows how special she is? How important she is?

NINE

It's like I was telling Jo, you know Jo. Gwen's daughter, works in despatch, always sits next to Bekki and Tyler in the canteen. Lives with him out of HR, not that they are married of course. Anyway, it doesn't matter, I was telling Jo how we hoped to have you back on your feet and at work as soon as possible. She didn't ask of course, no one has asked about you. Don't you think that's odd? I mean, you have portrayed yourself as this linchpin for years and the place is still running, better than ever really. There is no collection or get well soon card doing the rounds. The world is still spinning without you. How does that make you feel? Because I feel fantastic.

There was a collection, a card and even some very nice flowers. I was given them all last week as well as messages of love and well wishes to pass on. I left the flowers on the junction where those two smackheads crashed the other week. The card went in the bin outside the offie and the cash was spent inside on a very nice bottle of red. I had myself a lovely evening while she lay in bed sobbing and shivering.

The doctors went and changed my painkillers. Apparently, they were quite addictive, and they wanted to avoid any issues further down the line for me. It was all done in my best interest, after all I've been through enough haven't I?

Cold turkey really doesn't look pleasant, but her suffering was neither here nor there as far as I'm concerned. It was a very tough call, but in the end, I didn't want to be going out and getting skag for her every day. Feeding an addiction is a lot of commitment and she just really wasn't worth the time or effort when it came down to it. I don't like making decisions on the fly, or acting on impulse. I like to take my time and think things through but this time my heart overruled my head and I've really painted myself into a corner.

The last few weeks I've been taking sick notes into work for her that I've been writing myself. You really can buy anything online, and I could keep doing that, I guess. But sooner or later someone is going to want to see, God knows why. It's just inevitable, isn't it? I've already left it too late to play the grieving child, she's starting to stink. I could keep her in the bath and just hose her off every day. I guess that could work. It would save on washing anyway. Dad slabbed over the garden to stop me wrecking the flowers with my football so I can't bury her under the cover of darkness. The only logical option left is to report her missing and dump her somewhere she won't be found for a long long time. It's that or get caught or hand myself in and confess to it all. No matter what I do next, the end is fast approaching whether I like it or not.

They used to tell me they were going to take me back to where I came from. They used to tell me they were going to leave me in the woods for the bears to get me. They would tell me they were going to sell me to anyone who would have me. It's not that they didn't love me in their own special, different, ways. They saw how other parents spoiled and raised their kids to believe they were special and could do anything they wanted. They wanted to keep me grounded. They wanted me to know my place in the world. This is how I thrived in the ways I have. How I know the things I know and do the things I do. None of this is my fault. I'm the real victim here. I want you to remember that. I need you to remember that.

If you want to create a fake profile on some scummy site or even a whole new persona you need to start with the name. You'll always be tempted to go flamboyant and call yourself something like Ricardo Jareth or Danny Quatro, but these will raise suspicion from the off. Your new name needs to be as bland and as boring as you can muster. Don't use one you have already heard or try to borrow it off someone you know - you'll be busted before you even get going. Avoid alliteration, this isn't a comic book or some cheesy movie - no one is really called Vicky Vale or Sue Storm or Babe Bennett. Pick something memorable but not too memorable. You almost want to be as forgettable as possible.

Once you have a name you need a back story, you need a life you have already lived. You're not any type of hero and unless you know a considerable amount about serving, you certainly aren't any type of veteran. Don't paint yourself out to be anything of any use to someone. If you say you're a vet and their dog gets sick you're going to get a phone call. As boring as an accountant is, you don't want to be doing anyone's books. Pick a factory, work on a production line, in a store, drive a taxi. Make it mundane, make it vague but most of all make it believable.

If this is just an online gig, you'll need pictures. There are a few rules here. Don't go too attractive, but don't go too ugly either. Don't pick anything from the first few pages of a search result and don't ever steal pictures from an open social media account with more than fifty followers. If at all possible, avoid a face picture altogether, use a sunset, sunrise, the beach, a cute dog, kittens, cocktails - anything slightly twee works really. But never use a philosophical or inspirational quote on a black background, you'll just come across like a tosser.

This is how Darcy has come to believe she is meeting Leopold Lavinski. An immigrant from an as yet undecided eastern european country who is a primary school teacher by trade, but is here picking fruit to help out his family back home. Leopold is engaged to be married but is very lonely over here and is looking for some company.

Be open and honest about your intentions from the off. Unless it is your aim, you don't want anyone falling in love with you. Play it cool, don't be too eager, and don't go sending nude pictures unless you have a big stash built up that are all of the same body. Don't go fishing for compliments or information. Be aloof. Be mysterious, be nonchalant.

I was none of those things and that's where I went wrong. I was too desperate, too eager, too needy. I went to her when she should have come to me. She's more than just a prostitute, another girl stood on a corner looking for a quick few quid. She advertises herself, or is advertised, all across the internet if you know where to look. And I do know where to look. I am in all of these places as well under various aliases.

My favourite is the swinging website where I have managed to verify and even recommend myself to others using a handful of make-believe deviants. At times it's a bit like spinning plates but the end result is nearly always worth it.

It's there that I found one of them from that night. The one who swung the first punch. The one who started the ball rolling. He calls himself TDH, Tall Dark and Handsome. He is none of those things, but are any of us really who we say we are? He says he is dom and is very experienced with bondage. He isn't either of them either. He is just another impotent little fat man with a taste for violence throwing his weight around. His is the classic story of someone who peaked in their youth and has been chasing that high ever since. He tells you stories of all the tries he scored and trials he had. He could have gone pro if it wasn't for his knee. I took a note of that. You always need to be paying attention to what is going on. Always look for the finer details. Sometimes what they don't say is important but more often than not people can be read like a book.

He messaged me first, which I liked

to be honest. He thought he was talking to Susie, a somewhat naive nineteen-year-old who was looking to experiment and broaden her horizons. He asked me if I had ever been spanked and I told him no one had ever laid a finger on me like that. The next message was a picture of his flaccid little cock. His hand cupping his balls, desperately trying to add an inch that just wasn't there, and to squeeze some life into the poor thing. This was when I knew I had him exactly where I wanted him.

We have messaged back and forth for a while. I flit between all but ignoring him and begging him for more. He has told me all of the things he wants to do to me and I have never told him any of the things that are going to happen to him. I have saved all of his pictures, told him I was taking screenshots of them so I could enjoy them later. What I did was send them all and a few select highlights of his missives to his wife, his mother, the headteacher at the school he taught at and the local press.

He has booked a hotel on the other side of town under an obviously fake name and will be getting there first. I'll message him full of apologies about how I'm running late but will be there as soon as possible. The original plan was to see how long I could string him along for and then just never turn up. But something has changed, and I'll soon find myself tottering down the hall towards room 237.

The lights will be out, and the door unlocked as per our agreement. I'm four hours late and fast running out of cleavage shots to send him. He's on the bed naked and ready to go as per the dozens of pictures he has sent me. I close and lock the door behind me, apologise for being so late but promise I'll more than make it up to him. He'll grunt something or other of no importance and go to come to me. I'll tell him to stay put and to close his eyes. I'll tell him his time will come soon, but first I have a little treat for him.

He'll start groaning as soon as he feels my weight on the mattress. He'll reach out for me and I'll playfully, but firmly, slap his hands away and tell him to keep still. To keep very, very still. I'll straddle his chest, pinning his arms to his side with my knees. Leaning in close so he can feel my hot breath on his ear. I'll whisper, all sultry like, that I'm going to give him the time of his life and then push the blade into his throat.

Once I'm sure he is definitely gone and I'm fully satisfied, I'll give him a final, lingering kiss, climb off him and put the lights on to admire my handiwork. It won't be neat, but it will be beautiful. He'll have ejaculated across the back of my leg and I'll need a much-deserved shower. I'll lick my lips and taste blood. For once in my life it won't be mine.

No. No. No. No. No. No. No. No. No. It won't work. It won't work. It won't work. It won't work. Where is the blade going to come from? How am I going to get in and out of the hotel with no one seeing me? Everywhere has cameras. Should I wear a disguise? I could put the blade in Mother's carry-on case with the other goodies that I could use on him. But then I'd have to unzip it and get it out and it needs to be spontaneous. What if he fights back? He's going to fight back. Any normal person would fight back. I could tie him to the bed and set the bed on fire. Set the hotel on fire. Burn the place to the ground. They'll have alarms, anyone who is able to will be able to get out without getting hurt. Only those who can't, won't, and it's them that deserve it. I could stay behind, hide in a cupboard so they never find me.

TEN

It's Darcy I'm meeting. Not Tessa or Dawn or Donna or Mandy. Darcy. Darcy from the landing. Darcy from the street corner. Darcy from the internet. Darcy. Not Tessa or Dawn or Donna or Mandy. Darcy. Darcy. Keep thinking about her name. Darcy. Don't think of the things they call her. Don't think of the things they have done to her. Don't think of the things she has been reduced to. Think of the person she is. Think of the person she could be. Darcy.

I've not been to work the last couple of weeks. I told them that I need to stay at home and look after Mother. I said how her condition was deteriorating rapidly and now someone needs to be there 24/7 for her. They were very understanding and told me to take all the time I need. All I had to do was ask and they would do anything they could. It's not all that much of a lie. I am pretty much here 24/7 as I'm terrified of someone finding her, finding us, and the whole world falling in on me. At times I can convince myself that I haven't actually done anything that illegal. It's not like I have killed anyone. Mother took my medication, anything that happened to her was her own doing. I'm the victim here. None of the email addresses I have used for my online fun and games are linked to each other or are logged in on any of my devices. So they would have to try really hard to link me to anything and it's not like I even tried to blackmail him. I'm the victim here.

Even if they do manage to prove something, no matter how tenuous it is, I'll just hide behind PTSD. I'll go to the papers and say they are harassing me. If the papers start hounding me, I'll go to the police and say they are harassing me because I wouldn't speak to them. I'm the victim here. No matter what any of them try to do, I'll still win in the end. Even if it means taking them all down with me. It's not like I have got anything to lose.

Darcy was coming round at half seven. Out-calls are more expensive, but I can't risk leaving Mother on her own or being seen out and about. Out-calls are more expensive but she's worth it. I finally got round to hosing Mother down and put her in the shed at the bottom of the garden for the evening. I changed the bedding, opened the windows, sprayed a load of air freshener, and I can't decide if the stench has gone or if it is just wishful thinking.

I was worried she would recognise the address, but then again, it's been years since she was here last. I don't want to think about all of the people she has seen between now and then. She's better than that. She's better than all of them. All I wanted to do was talk to her. That was true on that night and it's still true now. It isn't illegal to talk to people. Nobody can go to prison for just talking. Can they? She thought she was meeting Leopold Lavinski. Pretending to be someone else isn't very illegal. It's not like I've been doing any real serious fraud with it. People give fake names all the time and really what is a name anyway? You're never under any obligation to tell anyone the truth if you don't want to. They were always very open with me that I wasn't their child. Well sometimes dad was my dad, but mother was never my mum. Sometimes they had taken me in out of the goodness of their own hearts. Other times they fought tooth and nail to get me. Their version of the truth depended on how much they wanted to hurt me or butter me up at the time. The favourite one seemed to be that my real mum was a useless, good for nothing whore. I was always told that if I didn't buck my ideas up I'd end up on the street like her. Her drink and drug addictions were the reason I look like I do and why I'm not so smart. One time they told me I had come from a Romanian orphanage. Really, it's no wonder I have never felt like I have belonged anywhere. I've been disposable my whole life, no matter what the real truth is.

Darcy was bang on time. Just like the reviews said she would be. She came trotting down the path with a carry-on case full of toys, restraints and outfits like an echo from my childhood. When I made the booking, I explained how I was very shy and that the front door would be open. She let herself in and headed up the stairs where she was expecting to find me waiting for her in the bedroom. As she went upstairs calling out my new name, I left the kitchen, locked the front door and followed her upstairs.

We met on the landing and I made her jump. She apologised and said she was looking for Leopold. I apologised and said that he wasn't home yet, but she could stay and talk with me until he got back. She was trying not to stare, trying to pretend that she didn't recognise me. She was trying to look like she wasn't terrified. I told her I just wanted to talk. All I have ever wanted to do is talk.

She told me that the boys were waiting outside for her. I asked her, asked her, not to lie to me. I told her I knew she had driven here on her own.

She told me that if she didn't ring in an hour, they would be coming to get her. I told her that we better get started then. She asked me what I wanted from her and I told her, again, that I just wanted to talk. I said we didn't even have to do it in the bedroom. I told her that we could go back downstairs and sit in the living room. We didn't even have to sit next to each other.

Everything was moving too fast. It was all unravelling. She was scared and I didn't want her to be scared. I wanted her to feel safe. I hadn't spoken to anyone for this long in months and my jaw was starting to hurt. My head was starting to hurt. My head always hurt. It was like I was in a vice, but also that my brain was too big for my skull. I told her I would go downstairs first. I even offered to carry her case for her. All she had to do was follow and then listen and then she could go. That's all I wanted from her. That's all I wanted from anyone.

I waited in the hall until I heard her coming down the stairs. She was hugging the wall, trying to stay as far from me as she could. I went into the living room and heard her try the door then heard her start to sob when she realised it was locked and that she wasn't going anywhere soon. I wanted to comfort her. To go and hold her and tell her everything was going to be okay. But I couldn't. I could never lie to her. Never.

She came into the living room and started pulling her clothes off telling me that I had won and that she just wanted to get this over with. I told her that I just wanted to talk to her. I just needed to talk and for someone to listen. No one ever listens to me. Why won't anyone ever listen to me? She looked at me as if I was insane and pulled her knickers back up. She looked at her watch and told me to hurry up and all of a sudden, I didn't know what to say any more.

I should have asked her if she remembered me. Not from that night but from that day on the landing. I should have asked if she remembered the house. It's not like we had decorated, we're not made of money unlike people like Kelvin. I should have asked her if she noticed that our eyes are the same colour. I could have taken the opportunity to find out if she is really called Darcy. Instead I said nothing. I sat there and started to cry. Once the tears came, they wouldn't stop. They couldn't stop. I let it all out. I felt like I was deflating. Everything was slipping away, and I knew the game was up. I had my chance and I bottled it again. I was the pathetic loser I was always told I was. I clenched my teeth and swallowed whatever it was that crumbled inside my mouth. I wiped the tears and snot away and told her the keys were on the mantle. I told her to go. To leave and never look back.

She stood and sort of hovered for a few minutes and I realised that she still wanted, and needed, paying. I pulled the wedge of notes from my pocket and tossed them onto the coffee table. She started to count out what she said she was owed and I told her to take it all and just leave. She shrugged her shoulders and went.

I sat there in silence and waited for her to come back. I couldn't decide if I wanted her to come back alone and let me say what I needed to or to come back with the boys and finish the job once and for all. She never came. No one came. There were no sirens. The phones never rang. The silence was deafening. I sat there until the darkness came and I felt the emptiness sink back into place. I sat there until I felt worthless again.

I had a lot of things to do but no energy or inclination to do them. I needed to get Mother in from the shed. She'd be hungry and tired. I could ring the doctors tomorrow and ask them to come look at her. I could tell them I have been struggling and didn't know what to do anymore. It wouldn't even be a lie. Mother is a proud woman she wouldn't dare tell them what I had done to her. What had happened in her house. Every family has their secrets and hidden shames. We could spin some dramatic recovery story for work, and they would happily buy it. Give it eight months and it will be like none of this ever even happened. Give it eight years and I'll struggle to tell you what was and what wasn't real. I just need to make the first move.

I yawn and stretch. Something breaks off inside me. I run my tongue over my ragged teeth and wonder how long I have left. I wonder how long any of us have left. I lick my lips and taste blood.

ABOUT THE AUTHOR

They say to write what you know. James Josiah doesn't know who "they" are, but they seem to know what they are talking about, so he goes along with it anyway.

With this in mind, he likes to write about depression and music.

To date, he has written: Days of Madness, which captures a month-in-the-life of a manic-depressive, C90 – a story about mixtapes and unrequited love, and Stay Happy – a story about love that isn't a love story, and is more about how you shouldn't feed ducks bread.

He likes pina coladas and getting caught in the rain. He does, however, dislike talking about himself in third person.

https://www.facebook.com/jamesjosiahauthor/